To Gill, my best friend ~ A B

To Julia, thank you for your support
and patience ~ T B

LITTLE TIGER PRESS LTD,
an imprint of the Little Tiger Group
1 Coda Studios, 189 Munster Road, London SW6 6AW
www.littletiger.co.uk
First published in Great Britain 2018
This edition published 2019

Text copyright © Anna Bowles 2018
Illustrations copyright © Tim Budgen 2018
Anna Bowles and Tim Budgen have asserted their right to
be identified as the author and illustrator of this work under
the Copyright, Designs and Patents Act, 1998

There once was a miller who had three sons. When he died, everything he owned was split between them.

The **eldest** son got the mill.

The **middle** son got the donkey.

The **youngest** son got . . .

This STUPID cat!

"I'm a very clever cat," said Puss. "I'll prove it if you bring me three things.

A bag made of fine velvet.

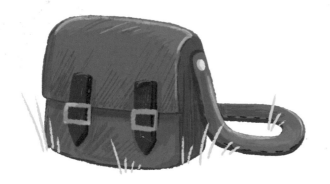

Boots made of soft leather.

And a hat with a fancy, red feather."

"How will that help *me*?" grumbled the cat's master. Still, he did what Puss asked him to.

There's a good boy!

Nearby, rabbits were jumping
and bouncing around.

Puss soon trapped one.

The clever cat dragged his bag up to the castle.

"Your Majesty, I bring you a rabbit from my master."

"And who is he?" replied the King.

Then Puss told a whopper lie.

His name is Lord Carabas.

Puss went back out to hunt.
    Chickens were strutting and flapping
around the yard. Puss soon trapped one
and took it to the King.

SQUAWK!

Day after day, Puss brought more . . .

. . . and more and MORE gifts.

The King grew very fat and very pleased with Lord Carabas.

One morning the King said to his daughter, "What a lovely day. Let's drive to the river and get some fresh air."

Puss dragged his master down to the river. "Take off your clothes!" he cried. Then Puss shoved him SPLASH! into the water.

The King's driver pulled Master out of the lake.
Puss was worried about his master's worn-out
shirt and torn trousers. No lord would wear those.
So Puss hid them!

"Someone has stolen my master's fine clothes!"
Puss wailed.

The King tutted and said, "How awful to rob an honest man like that. Driver! Fetch robes for Lord Carabas."

Then he asked Puss's master, "Will you join us for a drive?"

Puss ran ahead and found some women gathering corn.
    "Hey, you!" cried Puss. "Tell the King that these
fields belong to Lord Carabas. Or I'll chop you up
like mincemeat!"

"Whose field is this?" asked the King when he came along.

It belongs to Lord Carabas, Your Majesty!

"What fine lands you have,"
said the King to Puss's master.

Around the corner a shepherd was herding sheep.

"Hey you!" cried Puss. "Tell the King that these sheep belong to Lord Carabas. Or I'll shred you to ribbons!"

GRRRRRr!

The frightened man did as he was told.

Puss did the same thing again,

and again,

Run!

and again.

Ahhh!

Finally Puss came to a castle. "That's the ugliest castle I've ever seen!" Puss laughed. "But it will be the perfect home for my master."

The ogre was excited to have visitors and started boasting, "I'm a magician! I can change myself into any kind of creature."

"I don't believe you can turn yourself into a lion," said Puss.

Puss was so terrified that his fur stood on end and his hat and boots jumped off!

"You are very FIERCE and SCARY," said clever Puss. "But FIERCE and SCARY is easy. It's much harder to be small and quick."

"Ha!" grunted the ogre. Then he changed into a mouse.

TA-DA!

"You're not as quick as me!" cried Puss.

He jumped on the mouse
and ate him up.

YUM!

"That's that," said Puss.
"Now I think this castle
needs a new owner."

When the King came along, Puss ran out of the castle gates.

"Welcome to the castle of Lord Carabas!" he said.

"Does all this belong to you?" the King asked Puss's master.

"Do you think I'm pretty?" the Princess asked.

That very day the lord and the princess were married. And what about Puss?

Puss became a great lord too, with fine clothes, fine food and a feather bed to sleep on.

He even gave up chasing mice.

Mostly.

Eeeek!

FAIRYTALE CLASSICS

are familiar, fun and friendly stories – with a marvellously modern twist!

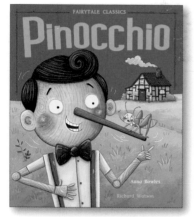

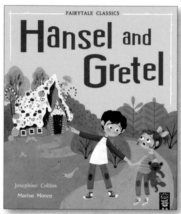

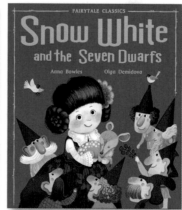

For information regarding any of the above titles
or for our catalogue, please contact us:
Little Tiger Press Ltd, 1 Coda Studios,
189 Munster Road, London SW6 6AW
Tel: 020 7385 6333 • E-mail: contact@littletiger.co.uk
www.littletiger.co.uk